BUNNY CHRISTMAS

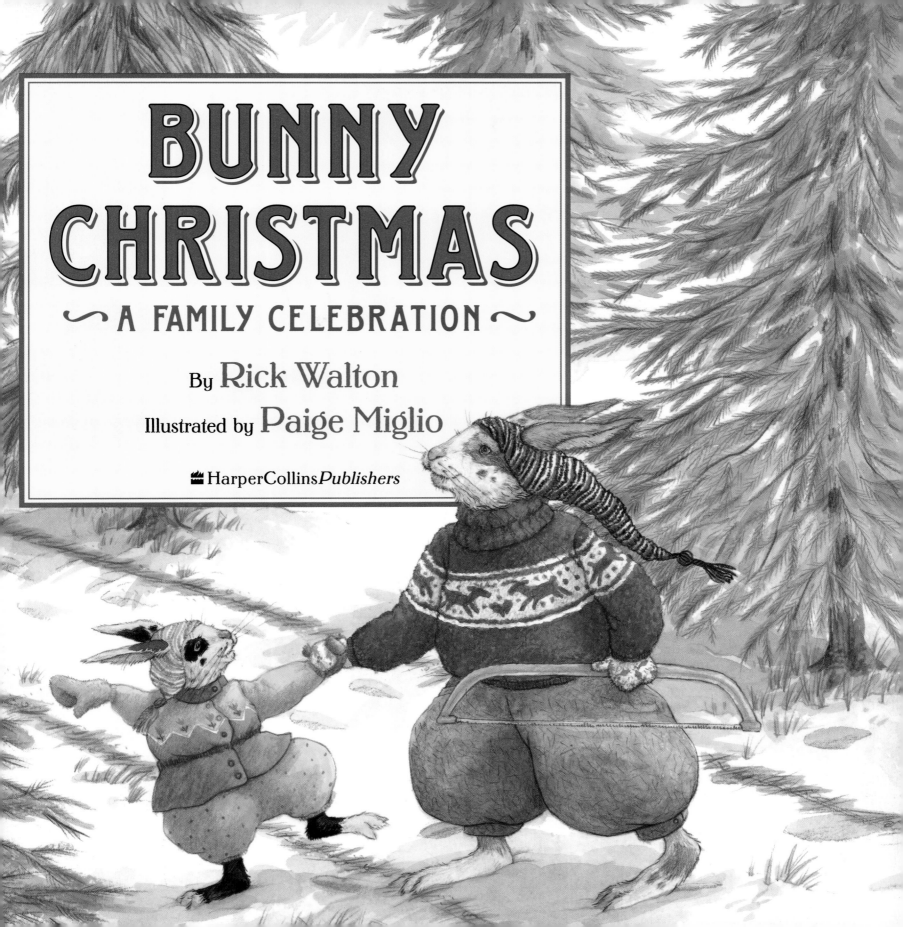

BUNNY CHRISTMAS
~ A FAMILY CELEBRATION ~

By Rick Walton

Illustrated by Paige Miglio

HarperCollins*Publishers*

To the Ray and Maribeth Ivie family,
who carry the Christmas spirit year round.
—R.W.

For Judi
—P.M.

Bunny Christmas: A Family Celebration
Text copyright © 2004 by Rick Walton
Illustrations copyright © 2004 by Paige Miglio
Manufactured in China by South China Printing Company Ltd.
All rights reserved.
www.harperchildrens.com

Library of Congress Cataloging-in-Publication Data
Walton, Rick.   Bunny Christmas : a family celebration /
by Rick Walton ; illustrated by Paige Miglio.   p.   cm.
Summary: An extended family of rabbits enjoys preparing for Christmas
together.   ISBN 0-06-008415-4 — ISBN 0-06-008416-2 (lib. bdg.)
[1. Christmas—Fiction.   2. Rabbits—Fiction.   3. Family life—Fiction.
4. Stories in rhyme.]   I. Miglio, Paige, ill.   II. Title.
PZ8.3.W199 Btu   2003   [E]—dc21   2002005941

Typography by Carla Weise
1 2 3 4 5 6 7 8 9 10 ❖ First Edition

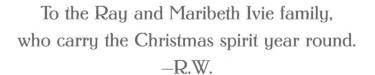

Christmas is coming. There's joy in the air.
And bunnies are hopping about to prepare
To welcome their relatives and see everyone,
For this is the season for family and fun.

Christmas is coming. The bunnies string chains
Of popcorn and paper, and hang candy canes.
Mother and daughter and son trim the tree,
Then Mom sets the star on the top—carefully.

Christmas is coming, and Father hangs lights
To brighten the world on cold winter nights.
The kids and their dad put a wreath on the door,
Some evergreen boughs at the windows, and more.

Christmas is coming. With planning and care,

Gift-making bunnies work hard everywhere.

Sister is making a present for Brother,

And one for her father, and one for her mother.

Christmas is coming. With paper and glue,

Brother bunny makes beautiful cards, quite a few.

A card for his sister, some cards for his kin,

Cards to put holiday messages in.

Christmas is coming, and bunny kids go
To play with their cousins out in the white snow.
A snow battle brews, the snowballs pile high,
While in the soft snow, the snow angels fly.

Then Grandpa takes bunnies, bundled and wrapped,

Bunny paws mittened, and heads stocking-capped,

To ski and to sled down steep snowy hills.

They all enjoy racing and laughter and spills.

Christmas is coming. Roll out the sweet dough
And cut cookie shapes. Then in the trays go.
Then Grandma makes candy and sweet, berry pies,
And grandchildren help her with wide, hungry eyes.

Christmas is coming, and two bunnies go

With their aunt to see Santa. He shouts, "Ho, ho, ho!"

A good niece and nephew pet all the reindeer

And whisper their wishes into Santa's ear.

It's now Christmas Eve. Uncle Bunny is here
Directing the pageant put on every year
With shepherds and wise men and cattle and sheep,
A mother, a father, and baby asleep.

Then bunnies share hugs and good wishes and food,

While carolers add to the holiday mood,

For everyone hopes that this joy never ends:

A big happy family of neighbors and friends.

It's now Christmas morning. Young bunnies go see
What Santa Claus left for them under the tree.
And Brother and Sister, Father and Mother,
Empty the stockings they filled for one another.

Then cousins, aunts, uncles, and grandparents, too,
Arrive to share dinner, as families do.
They eat and they laugh and enjoy, every one.
It's Christmas, the season for families and fun.

Grandmother Grandfather Grandmother

Aunt Uncle Father Mother

Cousins Sister Brother

Dear Everyone

We are havi
a wonderful tin
wish
with
Sant
gift
nd
ki

With lo

Gra

Pop